Some
Secrets
Hurt

Visit us at ShadowMountain.com

Library of Congress Cataloging-in-Publication Data
Garner, Linda Kay.
   Some secrets hurt : a story of healing / by Linda Kay Garner; illustrated by D. Brandilyn Speth.
      p. cm.
   Summary: Maggie is upset because someone she knows has been touching her in a way that makes her uncomfortable and says that she must keep it a secret, but she finally decides to tell her parents. Includes parents' guide.
   ISBN 978–1–60641–135–3 (paperbound)
   [1. Child sexual abuse—Fiction. 2. Secrets—Fiction.] I. Speth, D. Brandilyn, ill. II. Title.
   PZ7.G18423Som 2009
   [E]—dc22   2009005708

Printed in the United States of America
Publishers Printing, Salt Lake City, Utah

10   9   8   7   6   5   4   3   2   1

Some Secrets Hurt

A Story of Healing

Written by Linda Kay Garner

Illustrated by D. Brandilyn Speth

SHADOW
MOUNTAIN ®

Salt Lake City, Utah

Maggie has a secret.

Some secrets feel good inside,

like a birthday surprise,

or doing a good deed,

or knowing something special.

Maggie's secret is not a happy secret, though.
It doesn't feel good inside. In fact, it hurts.

Sometimes Maggie has a sick feeling in her stomach.

Sometimes she feels sad,

or scared,

or angry.

Sometimes she wants
to run away and hide.

Sometimes she cries.

Maggie's secret makes her feel funny around grown-ups.

She doesn't know who to trust.

Maybe she can't trust anyone.

Maggie doesn't want to share her secret because it is embarrassing and personal. She doesn't want anyone to know. She thinks it is her fault. It's not Maggie's fault, but she doesn't know that.

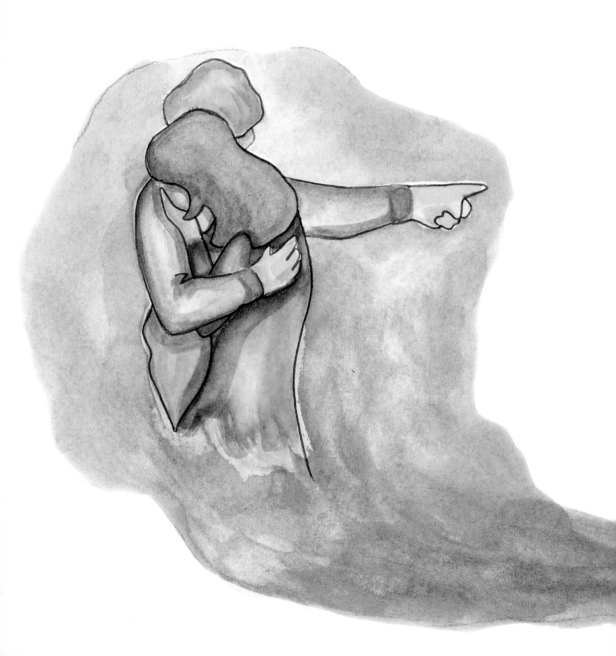

She is afraid to tell because she doesn't want to get in trouble. She thinks her mom and dad will be mad at her. She wonders if they will believe her.

Maggie knows all about strangers. She knows that some-times strangers can be dangerous. But Maggie's secret is not about a stranger. Maggie's secret is about someone she knows very well. Maggie's secret is about someone her whole family knows and trusts.

Strangers are not the only people who can be dangerous. Sometimes people we know can also be dangerous. Grown-ups are supposed to take care of children and protect them. Most grown-ups are kind and helpful to children, but not all grown-ups are kind to children.

If someone makes you feel uncomfortable, it is not your fault. If someone makes you feel uncomfortable, you should tell a grown-up that you trust. Usually your mom or dad is the person you should tell.

Someone close to Maggie has been touching her in uncomfortable ways. "Don't tell," he says. "If you tell, your parents will be mad at you."

Sometimes he gives her presents.

He tells her she is special.

He says, "This is our secret."

The touching doesn't feel right, and Maggie wants him to stop. She knows the touching is wrong, but she doesn't know how to make him stop.

There is only one way to make him stop.

Maggie must tell.

She is scared, but she knows what to do. It is hard to tell, but she is brave enough to do hard things.

Maggie tells her mom and dad. She knows they love her and she can trust them to take care of her. She wants to be in control of her own body. She needs help to make the touching stop.

Maggie has done the right thing. Her mom and dad are not mad at her. They believe her. They are proud of her courage. They hug her, and it feels good. This kind of touching is nice.

Maggie's mom and dad will protect her. They will make the bad touching stop. They will make him stop. They will get help so that he will not hurt anyone else. People who hurt children are sick and need help. Maggie's parents will make sure he gets help.

Maggie feels much better now. She still hurts inside, but she is going to get better. There are lots of kind grown-ups who will help her get better.

She feels stronger already.

What happened to Maggie is abuse. No matter what age you are, it is wrong for someone to touch you in ways that make you uncomfortable.

If this happens to you, it is not your fault. Talk to an adult you can trust to help you. Usually your mom and dad are the best ones to help you. You can also talk to a teacher or the parent of a friend. A church leader may also be a good choice.

No one should touch you underneath your underwear. No one should take pictures of you without your clothes. No one should try to get you to do things you don't want to do by giving you presents.

No one should tell you to keep secrets from your parents. A grown-up should not try to be alone with you.

You can trust your feelings. If you feel uncomfortable, that is your body telling you that what is happening to you is wrong. Have courage. Get away as soon as you can and tell someone. You will find that you can be very strong if you take charge of your own body, but you cannot do it alone. By telling, you can also protect other children from being abused.

You will start to feel better soon.

Parents' Guide

1. The only thing worse than finding out that your child is being sexually abused is not finding out.

2. Both boys and girls can be targets for sexual abuse. Age is not a factor. Young children and teenagers alike can be abused.

3. Most children are abused not by strangers but by someone they know and trust. Abusers have sometimes been a family member, a close friend of the family, a teacher, a coach, a camp counselor, or a baby-sitter. Abusers can be male or female. They can be any age, from other children to grandfathers.

4. Often children are afraid to tell. Their abusers warn them not to tell. In addition, children worry that they will be blamed. They wonder if it is their fault. They also worry that no one will believe them.

5. Beware of anyone who showers your child with gifts or favors. Be especially wary of anyone who wants to spend time alone with your child.

6. Sometimes abuse starts out as tickling or wrestling and gets more intimate. Be certain your child can tell the difference. Make sure he or she knows which parts of his or her body are private. These parts may be simply defined as the parts of the body that are usually covered by underwear or a swimsuit.

7. Notice changes in behavior that might suggest sexual abuse, including nightmares, bed-wetting, withdrawing from friends or family, fear of being left alone, change in eating habits, avoiding relationships with others, unexplained sadness, or anger.

8. In teenagers, behavior changes may include avoiding dating, voicing an extreme dislike of the opposite sex, or expressing a desire never to marry. In extreme cases some teenagers turn to promiscuity, alcohol, or drugs as a result of sexual abuse. Another teenage sign of abuse may be anger or voicing self-injurious or suicidal thoughts.

What to Do?

1. Maintain a loving relationship with your child. Make it easy for your child to talk to you. Have frequent talks about all sorts of things, both important and unimportant. Be a safe person for your child to talk to.

2. Talk to your child about sexual touching. Ask if anyone has touched your child inappropriately. Remind your child that it is okay to say no to someone who wants to touch them inappropriately. Teach them to get away as quickly as possible, and always tell. The idea is not to frighten your child but to give enough guidance that your child will know what to do.

3. Always believe your child. Always remind your child that it was not his or her fault. Never blame your child.

4. Stay calm. If you overreact, your child may feel threatened or shut down. Thank your child for trusting you with the information. Tell your child he or she did the right thing by telling you and that now you will be able to help.

5. Some children may find it difficult to talk about sexual abuse but could draw a picture or write down a name.

6. Seek professional help from your family physician and contact the local authorities.

7. Support your child in his or her healing process, and do not blame yourself unnecessarily. Take whatever steps are needed to keep your child safe.

"Parents' Guide" and "What to Do" adapted from *To Strengthen the Family*, by JoAnn Hibbert Hamilton (Las Vegas: Positive Values Publishing, 2003); used with author's permission.